A story is a good way

to display deep truths

Not only children love stories

The TimeTunnel
STORY SONG

SHARON ANDERSON
Illustrated by Ollie Anderson
Artwork on Covers by Mantradevi Cicero

by Sharon Anderson
and illustrated
by Ollie Anderson

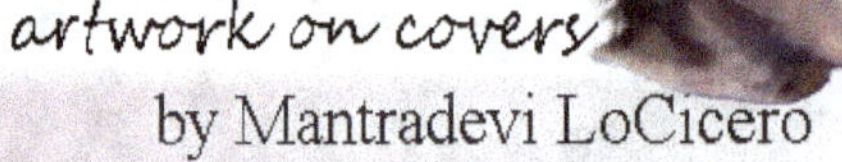

by Mantradevi LoCicero

adapted from

The Time Tunnel

book by

Swami Kriyananda

CRYSTAL CLARITY PUBLISHING

**the mp3 song companion
may be downloaded
free from the website
SharonLenoreAnderson.com
under the audiobooks tab**

For life's an idea
Like a lullaby song
Where in vibrations hum
Waves of feeling become
Tranquil ocean of calm
So with no-one to be then
And no essence to form

No distance for Time
To measure its line
Vast freedom is born

Lo - We only are a thought   A passing dream
Dissolving like a drop of rain into a stream
With nothing left of who we thought to be someone
Feel the heart expand and all there is become

The thrust behind vibration is Aware
The essence of Creation dwelling there

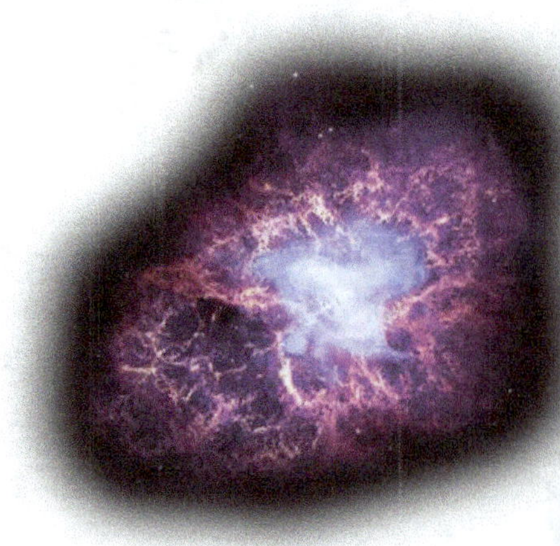

The Time Tunnel

story song

Here's told an adventure
Not so long ago
By a bold one who came
Molding iron's old age
To a dawning of Gold

As a boy in Romania
Nineteen twenty near five
Donny's dad drilled for oil
In that olden day soil
Where these truths came alive

$\mathcal{W}$ith Disney-like magic
The scenes did unfold
Only differencing slight
To parables like
The ones Jesus told

But if you listen closely
And you have eyes to see
We'll break through the light
Cross cosmos in flight
To the center of you and me

This Time Tunnel story
Started deep in the woods
Two brothers wondering
Stumbled upon something
Wondrously Good

An old laboratory
Had exploded and there
Was a tunnel behind
Where the boys were to find
They could go anywhere

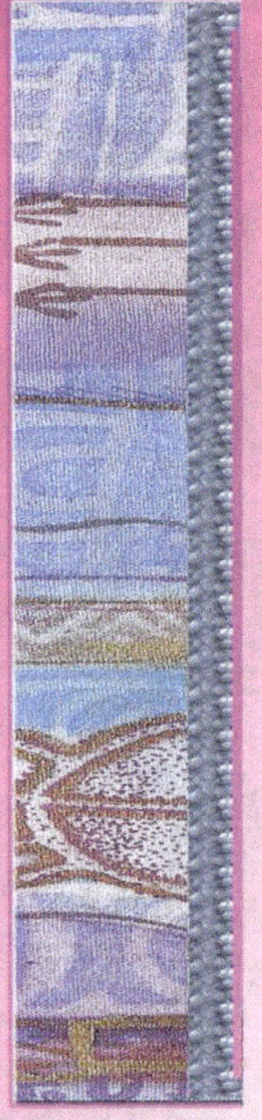

They even found traces
Where a barrier broke
Left flesh and bones
of a real dinosaur
In the time of our own

For as they would find out,
A young scientist was chased
They got going too fast,
And with a great Crash
The divide was erased

On we go   Through the tunnel they decided
Who would know   What awaited them inside

*L*ike entering into a cosmic brain
Where your very molecules   Orbiting beneath the skin
Mingled with the vastness of   Space
Where molten gases formed from nebuli
Lo – We only are a thought   A passing dream
Dissolving like a drop of rain into a stream
With nothing left of who we thought to be someone
Feel the heart expand and all there is become
The thrust behind vibration is Aware
The essence of Creation dwelling there

Little Donny and Bobby
Found they couldn't turn home
They were shrinking so fast
Dust like boulders passed
Falling toward the unknown

And so they just melted
In the light and the hum
And the energy surged
Until they emerged
With light spheres round each one

Now they join up with Hansel;
The Scientist's son
Here in this new world
Of travelling time
Where exploring is fun

And dear Reader, you know how
The day disappears
When the child is engrossed
"Now" is the host,
There's nothing but "Here"

Off they fly With their Time Light Spheres around them
Where Peasants rise   In the time of William Tell

*I*t was a dark age
Fifteen hundred or so
And the way people dreamed
Like concrete it seemed
Dogmatic and slow

But the sheer desperation
Made occasion to soar
And a man becomes brave
In his struggle to save
What we've all come here for

Shall we flee   To the realm of ancient Egypt
Lucky We   To get out of here alive!

For life's an idea
Like a lullaby song
Where in vibrations hum
Waves of feeling become
Tranquil ocean of calm

So with no-one to be then
And no essence to form
No distance for Time
To measure its line
Vast freedom is born

To see the beauty of the Pyramids
Is to know they were not made
By the slaves of a darker age
They serve to generate
GREAT   Power, Love and Wisdom
With astrological precision

In those days the rays of ancient Egypt rose above
Emanating waves of ancient Sages love
Reaching out to elevate Mankind
Galaxies like seasons mark the orbit of
That realm again   Within our reach   To find

Now onto Atlantis
And the future we go
Where they have discovered
Mechanical feats
Man still doesn't know

But I don't need to tell you
That it lies in the past
With the power man found
In oppression it drowned
For it just couldn't last

Bigger Better More and more I must have
Strangled them whose prisoner was their "Gain"

On into the future
Continue the line
Where Utopia lies
But it's not very wise
For it's all in the mind

If you want to reveal it
In truth and in life
You must go within
Reason is dim
Intuition is wide

Nature's gifts Are not yours for the taking
But if you give You expand and share its life

Donnie, Bobby, and Hansel
Wanted not history's pride
But to penetrate life
Its joys and its strife
In the quiet countryside

And so we go back then
To a moment of need
Where suffering serves
To straddle that line
Where you strive to succeed

They found a poor woman
In a tumble-down hut,
Her kindly response
Was all that she wants
Is food for her young

Her husband off fighting
For William the Great
Who would conquer the west,
In Englands conquest,
For the worlds better fate

They lent their hand
And she was graced with new ambition
A job to land   As a soup chef for the King

Let's continue on and find the wonder of
The one thing in this life that's ours to find

Diogenes   Was a simple man and holy
He lived inside   And he only owned one tub
The king stopped by   To offer gems and money
And He replied   "You are standing in my sun".

They finally all travelled
To a nice future scene
Where Hansel could rest
At the welcome request
Of a girl's family

And Donny and Bobby
Sailed off to America
World War Two on their heels
They were never to see
The Time Tunnel again

And so like the hearts beat
All good stories must end
Just a sprinkling of light
Then that day becomes night
Never to be again

Donny as Kriyananda
Two thousand thirteen
In a blaze of white light
Bid all a good night
And departed the dream

Swami Kriyananda
May 19, 1924 to April 21, 2013

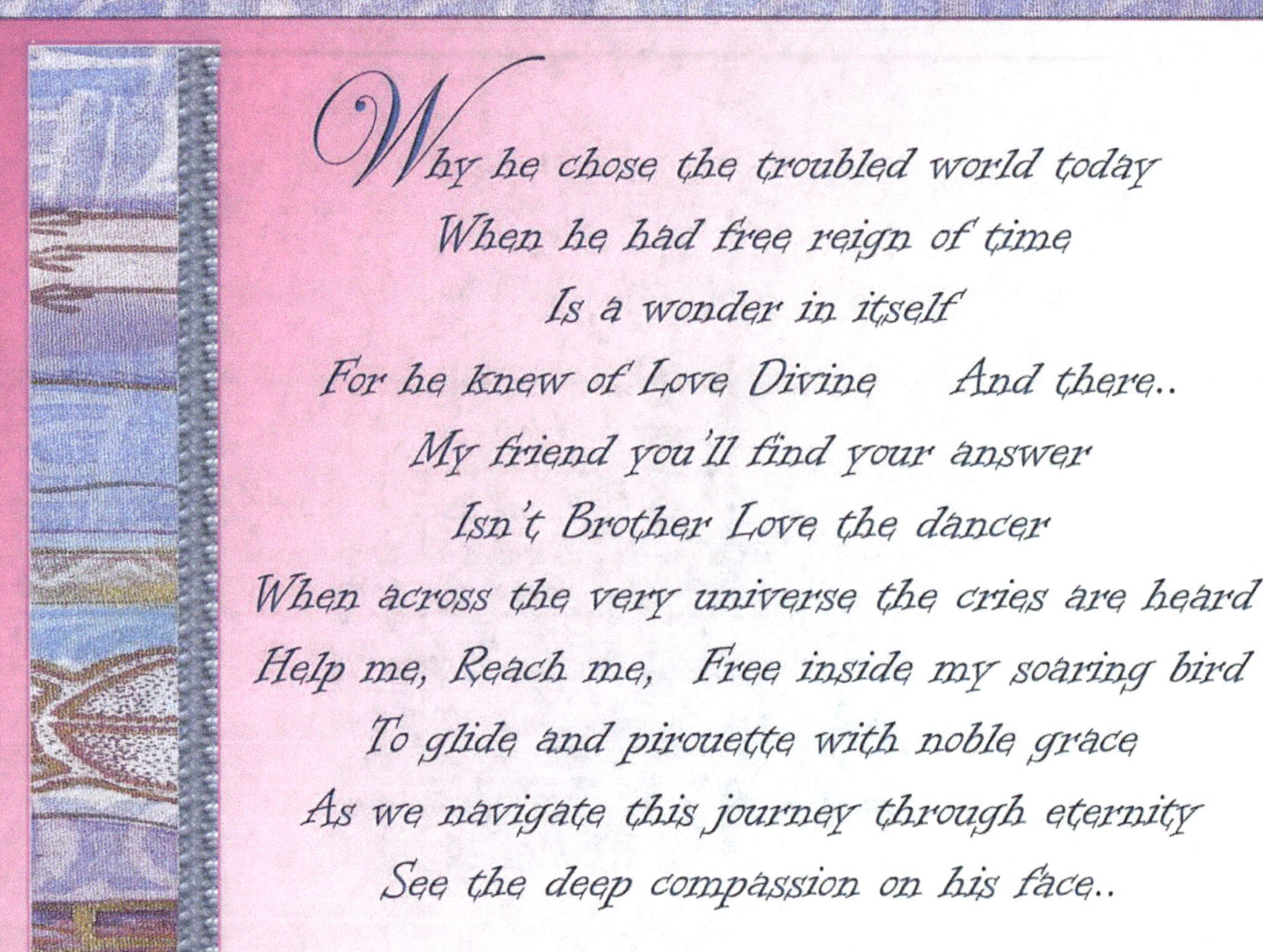

Why he chose the troubled world today
When he had free reign of time
Is a wonder in itself
For he knew of Love Divine   And there..
My friend you'll find your answer
Isn't Brother Love the dancer
When across the very universe the cries are heard
Help me, Reach me, Free inside my soaring bird
To glide and pirouette with noble grace
As we navigate this journey through eternity
See the deep compassion on his face..

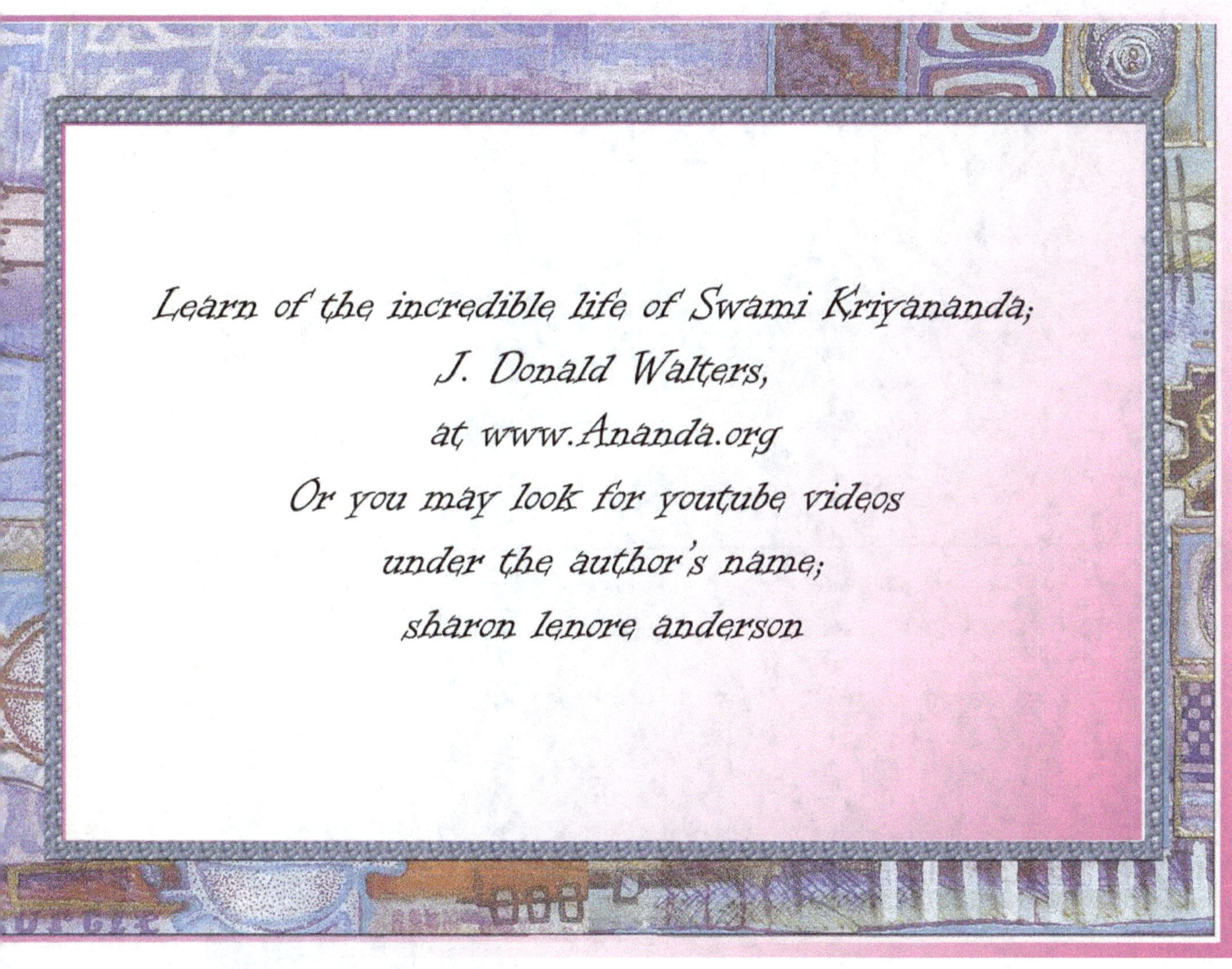

Learn of the incredible life of Swami Kriyananda;

J. Donald Walters,

at www.Ananda.org

Or you may look for youtube videos

under the author's name;

sharon lenore anderson

THE TIME TUNNEL

While exploring in Romania, brothers Donny and Bobby discover a ruined laboratory with a mysterious tunnel. Entering into it, their bodies shrink. They emerge into a beautiful countryside and meet Hansel, whose father invented the "time tunnel." After Hansel shows the boys how to encase themselves in time-light spheres, the trio journeys through time—visiting the Middle Ages, ancient Greece and Egypt, and forward into a surprising future. Along the way the boys gain valuable lessons about history, human behavior, and themselves.

"A charming tale that whisks the reader through time and space, imparting gems of wisdom along the way."

— Michael Sussman, author of the visionary novel, *Crashing Eden*

"Captivating and magical."

— Shankari Boldt, retired middle-school teacher

"*The Time Tunnel* will take you to Atlantis, ancient Egypt, and the future, as you never imagined them."

— Peggy Payne, author of *Sister India and Cobalt Blue*

"I think we've found another classic."

— Devi Novak, teacher, author of *Faith Is My Armor*

Swami Kriyananda is a direct disciple of the great world teacher, Paramhansa Yogananda. He has written more than 140 books, including *Stories of Mukunda* and *Education for Life*.

"A delightful tale that reveals spiritual insights through the innocent eyes of children . . . . Read this book to your children. Read it for yourself!"

— Jodine Turner PhD, bestselling author of the Goddess of the Stars and the Sea series, and *Carry on the Flame: Destiny's Call*

"Well written, gently spiritual, intellectually satisfying, and filled with fast-paced action, the book enters the imagination and stays there long after it is finished."

— Michael Gurian, bestselling author of The *Wonder of Boys, The Wonder of Girls, and The Miracle: A Visionary Novel*

"A wonderfully uplifting story that weaves adventure and timeless truths into a vibrant mosaic that will touch the heart and mind of readers of all ages."

— R. Daniel Noyes, author of *The Seven Doors*

"Transports the reader into a mystical realm some of us dream of exploring. We are gently reminded of our spiritual nature as we travel safely to other time and space 'realities.'"

— Caryn Colgan, artist, speaker, and author of *Ancient Pact: The Element of Air*

Crystal Clarity Publishers
800-424-1055
www.crystalclarity.com

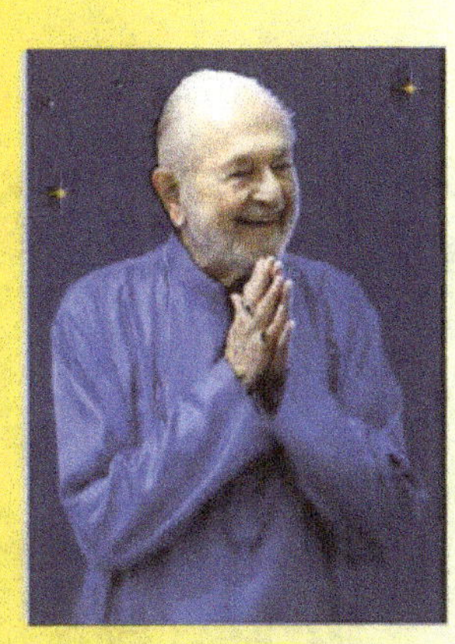

Swami Kriyananda is a world-renowned spiritual teacher and composer who has authored more than 140 books, including *Stories of Mukunda* (episodes from the boyhood of Kriyananda's guru, the great world teacher, Paramhansa Yogananda) and *Education for Life* (a treatise on modern education that serves as the foundation for the popular Living Wisdom Schools). Along with the Dalai Lama and Jane Goodall, Kriyananda is a member of the prestigious Club of Budapest. His autobiography, *The New Path*, won the 2010 Eric Hoffer Award.

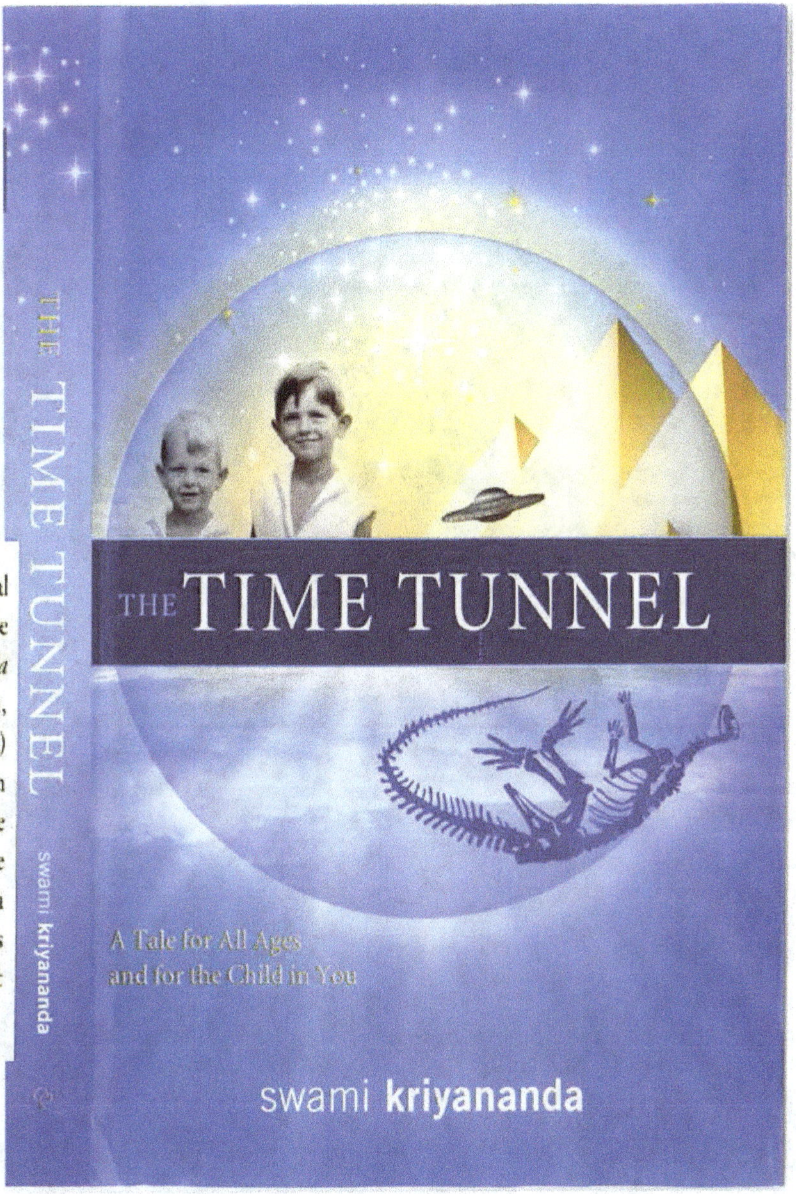
THE TIME TUNNEL
swami kriyananda
THE TIME TUNNEL
A Tale for All Ages
and for the Child in You
swami kriyananda

A thought from Sharon

As you can see , the original book is called "The Time Tunnel" by Swami Kriyananda. To me, the amazing thing about his story, is how it introduces such deep truths about nature and the universal structure.

That's why I love it so much.. that's why I wrote the song.

It is exciting and mind expanding, and even seems to reach out as if to touch the hem of the garments of recent and ancient sages alike-- to unveil intuitions that are coming of age. Some of these concepts can now be understood in our scientific realms. It is an astounding mind opener, and fun to read. And, irresistible, just like Swami himself.

My sister Ollie Anderson shares her wonderful artwork and helps to put Swami's story to song in a very dynamic and engaging way. You are sure to enjoy this timeless tale.

And, if it has intrigued the adventurer in you, here is a must for further reading:

Millions are wondering what the future holds for mankind, and if we are soon due for a world-changing global shift. Paramhansa Yogananda (author of the classic *Autobiography of a Yogi*) and his teacher, Sri Yukteswar, offered key insights into this subject. They presented a fascinating explanation of the rising and falling eras that our planet cycles through every 24,000 years. According to their teachings, we have recently passed through the low ebb in that cycle and are moving to a higher age — an Energy Age that will revolutionize the world. Over one hundred years ago Yukteswar predicted that we would live in a time of extraordinary change, and that much that we believe to be fixed and true — our entire way of looking at the world — would be transformed and uplifted. In *The Yugas*, authors Selbie and Steinmetz present substantial and intriguing evidence from the findings of historians and scientists that demonstrate the truth of Yukteswar's and Yogananda's revelations.

"An amazing, mind-expanding investigation of the hidden cycles underlying the rise and fall of civilizations. I found *The Yugas* not only intellectually convincing but also spiritually and emotionally uplifting and deeply healing as well. Despite the dark signs of the times we live in, there is hope here for all of us." —**Graham Hancock**, author of *Fingerprints of the Gods*

"The conventional mainstream view of an overall linear progression in human history is no longer tenable; it is now clear that the ancients of 10,000 to 15,000 years ago were not 'primitives' and we have much to learn from them. This is a profound book... It provides new revelations on the unfolding of human potential over the course of millenia." —**Robert M. Schoch, PhD**, author of *Pyramid Quest: Secrets of the Great Pyramid and the Dawn of Civilization*

"Selbie and Steinmetz have, in my opinion, produced a work of genius. If you aren't satisfied with what you've read, or been taught, about the linear development of civilization, you will find in this book an alternate picture of our Earth's history that will, I think, thrill you." —**Swami Kriyananda**, author of *The New Path*

"Move over Copernicus, another revolution is underway! *The Yugas* will not only change the way we look at history, it will change the way we see ourselves and the world around us. This is a wisdom whose time has come. The startling revelations and sweeping vision of Selbie and Steinmetz deliver a story so timeless it will challenge and inspire generations to come!" —**Walter Cruttenden**, author of *Lost Star of Myth and Time*

"Casts an important new light on the history and evolution of the human race and the mysteries of the great cycles of time that we must all honor. All those who want to understand our species and the hidden cosmic influences that govern our lives will benefit from its detailed examination. Those who study the book carefully will come away with a transformed vision of our world and its spiritual potentials." —**Dr. David Frawley (Pandit Vamadeva Shastri)**, author of *Astrology of the Seers* and *Yoga and Ayurveda*

Introduction

In 1905 Albert Einstein turned the world of physics upside down—
for the first time the world saw the now famous equation, $E=mc^2$.
Einstein fundamentally altered our understanding of the physical universe by proving that all matter was essentially condensed energy.

The nineteenth century view of the physical world was primar-
ily mechanical; all matter was considered solid and fundamentally
immutable. Although matter was considered to be made up of infini-
tesimally small objects, these were seen as solid objects nonetheless,
and were believed to obey the same basic laws as did the sun and the
planets. Time, too, was thought to be an unyielding constant through-
out the universe, unaffected by changing conditions. In the nineteenth
century the universe was seen as a very large machine, a clockwork of
infinite size, functioning precisely and inexorably in its slow grandeur.

Today we hold a very different view of the physical world. All matter is understood to be energy in a condensed form. Not only do we
consider matter mutable, we know that the tiniest atom is capable
of being transmuted into vast amounts of energy. Both the incred-
ibly destructive force of nuclear weapons, and the prodigious energy of
nuclear power, testify to the profound implications of the deceptively
simple equation $E=mc^2$.

Our view of the larger universe has also undergone a revolution. We
now know that objects in space do not move in straight lines—because
there *are* no straight lines. Space itself is curved and the universe is
finite. No physical object can go faster than the speed of light. The
speed of light is, in fact, the only constant in the universe—all else is
measurable only in relation to that constant. Even time is understood
to be relative to light.

The atom, previously conceived of as a constellation of tiny objects,
like a miniature solar system with the nucleus taking the place of the
sun (you probably made a model of one in sixth grade), has given way
to a concept that cannot even be visualized. Physicists now conceive of
the atom as a tiny area of space in which objects wink into and out of
the quantum, subatomic world—a world where the very act of trying

to observe the atom actually changes what is observed. Niels Bohr, the eminent early twentieth-century physicist and Nobel Prize winner, called the quantum world Potentia. Others have referred to it as quantum flux or quantum foam, an energetic maelstrom just below the threshold of measurable perception.

String theory, the latest "theory of everything," goes even further. String theory posits that there are no actual physical structures at all, that even the unimaginably small sub-atomic structures that physicists try to study, such as quarks, are, in reality, made up of even smaller vibrating strings and rings of energy.

Just a little more than a hundred years ago we understood our world to be made up of matter, interacted with by energy. Now we understand our world to be made up of energy, assuming the form of matter.

~~~~~~~~~

Acknowledgements

This book could not have been written were it not for Sri Yukteswar and Paramhansa Yogananda. Their twentieth century writings and teachings led the way in making the ancient teachings of India understandable to the Western mind. The significance of the yugas, in particular, had become lost in Indian tradition, but these two great souls presented the yugas anew, in simple clarity, giving them fresh relevance to our modern energy age.

This book also owes a great debt to the many talks and articles of Swami Kriyananda (J. Donald Walters) on the impact and qualities of the yugas. He has added rich dimension and depth of detail to our understanding of the yugas.

We would also like to acknowledge the legions of scientists and researchers willing to explore beyond orthodoxy—be they archeologists, professionals, and gifted amateurs alike, who are not satisfied with the standard linear theory of human development, or doctors and biologists, who are not satisfied with the standard material theory of human consciousness. Their dedicated work, and their thousands of books, articles, and lectures, present for all to see an astonishing number of unsolved mysteries of the ancient past, and fundamental gaps in our modern understanding of man.
~~~~~~~~~

Foreword
By Swami Kriyananda

I am sincerely pleased to be able to recommend this book, with enthusiastic applause. The subject has long interested me—indeed, from my youth. But I am deeply impressed by the depth of research and the astuteness with which the authors have approached their subject. I have written several books myself that included some of the points contained here, but this book goes far beyond my own minor contribution to the subject.

It was Swami Sri Yukteswar, in his book *The Holy Science*, who first propounded this revolutionary explanation for changes that have occurred in human consciousness over the centuries. I had already written a "source theme" in high school for my English class, when I was sixteen, which showed my fascination even then with ancient civilizations. Not to belabor what may seem a purely personal point of view, what interested me then, and what interests me as much today nearly seventy years later, is that I found the traditional explanation for ancient civilizations wholly unsatisfactory. It made (and makes) no sense to me for mankind to have spent many thousands of years as a "hunter and gatherer," and then suddenly to appear in a mere instant, so to speak, as the founder of great civilizations, complete with cities, industries, literature, education, and sophisticated cosmologies.

The name I chose for my source theme went something like this: "Ancient civilizations and their view of the universe." (I had wanted to study, further, what it was in those civilizations that had influenced people to develop those views, but here I was forced to admit failure; I could discover no such subjective influences.)

Mankind must, from the start, have had all the intelligence he needed to build cities and, with them, the appurtenances of a sophisticated civilization. Indeed, I'd read that the brain capacity of Cro-Magnon Man was larger than our own. And I wondered, on reading Egyptian history, how it happened that such a mighty civilization, after building the great pyramids, had descended to the level of mediocrity that has been evident in historic times. I simply wasn't convinced by the conclusions reached by the historians, developed from the data they had gathered. In fact, the more I read their conclusions, the more I inclined to agree with Napoleon's statement, "History is a lie agreed upon."

One thing that bothered me about the insights of so many historians, antiquarians, and other "specialists" was that they allowed facts to assume a separate reality of their own, seeming quite inadequate in their understanding of human nature. It was as if their approach to history had been only to gather those facts, but to make no attempt to place themselves actually in the shoes of the people they wrote about.

One wonderful thing about Sri Yukteswar's revelations (and to me they did in fact seem revelatory) was that he wrote at a time when a descending cycle of enlightenment—as described in this book—could be observed merging historically into an ascending cycle, and bringing radical change in human awareness with the birth of our present era, or *yuga*, of energy. Many facts of history over the last three thousand years are more or less known. Sri Yukteswar's explanation of those facts was, for me, deeply satisfying. This book presents his thesis with crystal clarity.

Selbie and Steinmetz have, in my opinion, produced a work of genius. They have gone, I think, as deeply into this subject as present-day knowledge permits. I am convinced that, living as we do in a cosmic environment, and one infinitely greater, therefore, than our environment on this little Earth, we are influenced also by that larger environment. We cannot but be affected: not only in our weather, but even in our consciousness. I am persuaded that many changes in human awareness take place not only because of the accretion of knowledge, but also in response to waves of conscious energy flowing into our planet from outside. For I believe that cosmic energy affects even human intelligence and awareness.

I am so enthusiastic on these points, indeed, that my very interest might induce me to repeat some of the points so excellently covered in this book! Let me therefore bow off the stage at this point, with only this comment: If you aren't satisfied with what you've read, or been taught, about the linear development of civilization, you will find in this book an alternate picture of our Earth's history that will, I think, thrill you.

Here are some other books
Sharon has written,
inspired also by the teachings of
Swami Kriyananda/Yogananda

you can find video, music,
and commentaries from Sharon
on the web at
www.youtube.com/SharonLenoreAnderson
www.SharonAndersonMusic.com
or www.SharonLenoreAnderson.com.

free audio readings and book song downloads available
under the audiobook tab. See full book slideshows
of all the books at the above youtube site also

THE THRUST BEHIND VIBRATION
IS AWARE
THE ESSENCE OF CREATION
DWELLING THERE